Mum's Late

Elizabeth Hawkins

Illustrated by Pamela Venus

Tamarind

Tamarind Ltd

Sponsored by **NASUWT**

It's time to go home.
Everyone's waiting.

"Start getting ready, Jerome," says Mrs Stuart. "Paul, look. I can see your mother outside."

"My mother is always first," says Paul proudly, as Mrs Stuart lets him out of the door.

"What's happened to your mother, Jerome?" asks Mrs Stuart.

"She's not here," says Jerome.

"I expect she's on her way," says Mrs Stuart.

"There's your brother
with his mountain bike, Emily.

"Put on your helmet
and remember to hold on tight,"
says Mrs Stuart.

"Is your mother here yet, Jerome?"

"No," says Jerome.

"She's taking her time then,"
says Mrs Stuart.

"Look, Sammy.
Isn't that your father waiting?"

"Goodness me, your shoe laces
are undone and he's in a hurry,"
says Mrs Stuart.

"Now, have you seen
your mother yet, Jerome?"

"No."

"I expect she's been busy today."

"There's Mrs Slater," says Mrs Stuart.
"Who does she mind?"

"Me!" shouts Jenny.

"And me," calls Shawn.

"Hello, Mrs Slater.
Jenny drew a lovely picture today.
It's for her mother...
Can you see that she gets it?"

"What do you think has happened
to your mother, Jerome?"

"I don't know."

"Don't worry.
I expect she's been held up,"
says Mrs Stuart.
"She'll be here soon."

"There's nobody left,"
says Jerome.

"Go and sit
in the book corner,"
says Mrs Stuart.
"Choose a book
and have a quiet read
while you wait."

"She's forgotten me," says Jerome,
"and gone away for ever."

"Mothers don't forget their children,"
says Mrs Stuart.
"She'll be here soon, you'll see."

"Perhaps she's been squashed
by an elephant," thinks Jerome.

"Or perhaps she doesn't want me anymore and she's gone to choose a new little boy."

"Look Jerome! Who is that
coming through the gate?"

"It's my Mum!… My Mum!"

OTHER TAMARIND TITLES

A Tamarind Book

Published by Tamarind Ltd, 1999

Text © Elizabeth Hawkins
Illustrations © Pamela Venus
Edited by Simona Sideri

ISBN 1 870516 40 0

Designed and typeset by Judith Gordon
Printed in Singapore